GOOD SPORTS

Riley FETTER, STAR SETTER

By J.L. Anderson
Illustrated by Karl West

Rourke
Educational Media
rourkeeducationalmedia.com

www.rourkeeducationalmedia.com

Edited by: Keli Sipperley
Cover layout by: Rhea Magaro-Wallace
Interior layout by: Kathy Walsh
Cover and interior illustrations by: Karl West

Library of Congress PCN Data

Riley Fetter, Star Setter / J.L. Anderson
(Good Sports)
ISBN 978-1-64369-047-6 (hard cover)(alk. paper)
ISBN 978-1-64369-091-9 (soft cover)
ISBN 978-1-64369-194-7 (e-Book)
Library of Congress Control Number: 2018955956

Printed in the United States of America,
North Mankato, Minnesota

Table of Contents

Chapter One
The New Kid

"Welcome to the team," I say to the new kid, Valmik. "I'm Riley Fetter. Some kids call me Star **Setter**."

"Hi," Valmik says. "What kind of a dog is a star setter?"

"Not a dog! I set the ball in the air for my teammates to hit," I say.

"Oh," he says.

"Do you like volleyball?" I ask.

"Volleyball is fine," Valmik says. "A joke club would have been better."

"Heads up!" I say. A ball

flies toward Valmik.

It's too late.

The ball bonks Valmik in
the forehead.

Chapter Two
Trying Again

Coach Goats checks on

him. He is okay.

I tap the top of my head.

"Don't worry. We all get hit

sometimes," I say.

"Hey Riley, is Principal Ponytail your dad?" Valmik asks.

"No. Why?" I ask.

Maybe the ball hit him harder than I thought.

Valmik laughs. "You and Principal Ponytail are both wearing ponytails."

"Ha, ha. We both wear our hair in a ponytail sometimes but I don't wear silly ties," I say.

Valmik does not laugh at my joke.

I take my place near the net. There are six of us on either side.

The other team **serves** the ball over the net.

Elliot catches the ball like
a football.

"Score!" Valmik says.

"The ball should not be held or carried," Coach Goats says.

"Oh," Valmik says again.

"Wrong sport," Elliot says.

She giggles with Valmik.

Chapter Three
Killing It

The other team serves again. The ball soars over the net. Valmik **bumps** the ball to me. I set it for Elliot.

"Kill it!" I yell as Elliot hits it over the net.

"What! Where's the roach?"

Valmik says.

The other team returns the ball. But our whole team is looking for a bug. The ball hits the court. They score a point.

"There is no roach," I say.

"Kill it means to **spike** the ball to the other side."

Valmik laughs. Everyone laughs except for me and Coach Goats.

We get back to the game. The other team serves the ball.

It flies over the net. Elliot bumps the ball to Valmik.

He falls to his knees to keep the ball from hitting the ground. Ouch. His knees are red.

"I should stick with jokes,"
Valmik says.

"You can practice both.
That was a nice try. Would
you like to borrow my knee
pads?" I ask.

Valmik nods.

Coach Goats smiles at me.

The game starts again. I
set the ball for Valmik.

"You got this," I say.

Valmik spikes the ball hard. It hits the net.

"You almost killed it like a roach!" I say.

This time we laugh together.

We are going to have a lot more fun with Valmik on our team.

Bonus Stuff!

Glossary

bumps (buhmps): Uses the forearm to bump the ball in the air to pass to a teammate.

serves (survz): Hits the ball into play at the start of a set or after a point is scored.

setter (SET-ur): The person on the team who gets the ball into position for a teammate to hit.

spike (spike): To hit a volleyball down and over the net with force so that it is hard to return.

Discussion Questions

1. What do you think was going through Riley's mind after meeting Valmik?

2. How did Riley react after Valmik hurt his knees? Do you think Riley showed good sportsmanship?

3. How do you think Riley feels about Valmik now?

Activity:
Balloon Practice

Practice how to serve, set, and spike with a balloon! A balloon moves slower in the air than a volleyball so it gives you a chance to practice your skills by yourself, with a friend, or in a larger group.

Supplies
- balloon (*you can try balloons of all sizes for a challenge*)

Directions
1. Blow up the balloon or several balloons. Make sure to tie each balloon tightly.

2. If solo, stand and work on serving, setting, or spiking the balloon. If two players, stand across from each other, and if in a larger group, form a circle to practice your skills.

3. Try to keep the balloon from hitting the ground! Give a point for a correct hit and try to see how quickly you can get to 21 points.

Writing Prompt

Rewrite this story from the point of view of the volleyball or come up with your own silly volleyball-themed story. Don't forget to include a few jokes!

About the Author

J.L. Anderson once fell to her knees to save the ball from hitting the ground in a volleyball game. She was not wearing knee pads. She loves to write and spend time with her husband, daughter, and dogs in Austin, Texas.

About the Illustrator

Karl West lives and works from a studio on the small island of Portland in Dorset, England. His dogs, Ruby and Angel, lie under his desk while he works, snoring away.